PUFFIN BOOKS

The Muscle Machine

Alexander McCall Smith lives in Scotland. He is the author of over thirty books, many of them for children. He is married to a doctor and has two daughters, Lucy and Emily. His hobbies include playing brass and other wind instruments.

The Muscle Machine

Alexander McCall Smith

Illustrated by
Terry McKenna

PUFFIN BOOKS

*This book is for William and
Kit Walmsley*

PUFFIN BOOKS

Published by the Penguin Group
Penguin Books Ltd, 27 Wrights Lane, London w8 5tz, England
Penguin Books USA Inc., 375 Hudson Street, New York, New York 10014, USA
Penguin Books Australia Ltd, Ringwood, Victoria, Australia
Penguin Books Canada Ltd, 10 Alcorn Avenue, Toronto, Ontario, Canada m4v 3b2
Penguin Books (NZ) Ltd, 182–190 Wairau Road, Auckland 10, New Zealand

Penguin Books Ltd, Registered Offices: Harmondsworth, Middlesex, England

First published by Hamish Hamilton Ltd 1993
Published in Puffin Books 1995
3 5 7 9 10 8 6 4 2

Text copyright © Alexander McCall Smith, 1993
Illustrations copyright © Terry McKenna, 1993
All rights reserved

The moral right of the author has been asserted

Filmset in Monophoto Baskerville

Printed in England by Clays Ltd, St Ives plc

Chapter 1

GORDON WAS NOT particularly strong.
It's not that he was weak – it's just
that there seemed to be lots of people
who were very much stronger than he
was. If he had to lift something heavy,
for instance, he often found it quite
difficult, and sometimes he would not
be able to lift it at all.

This did not worry him too much
until a boy called Ted came to
Gordon's school. Now Ted was quite
strong – at least he was quite a bit
stronger than Gordon. And Ted, I'm
afraid to say, was a bully.

1

The first time that Gordon saw Ted bullying somebody, he couldn't believe it.

"Don't push that person around," said Gordon indignantly. "Bullying isn't allowed in this school."

"Says who?" retorted Ted, turning to stare into Gordon's face.

"The rules say so," said Gordon.

"And who's going to stop me?" said Ted. "Are you?"

"Yes," said Gordon, stepping forward.

But Ted just laughed. "Well, this is what I think of you and your rules!"

And with that he pushed Gordon to the ground – right to the ground – and walked away.

Gordon was furious, but there was nothing very much that he could do. Ted was much stronger than he was and if he tried to use force to stop him bullying people then he would clearly get nowhere.

Then Gordon saw the advertisement. It was at the back of one of his father's magazines and he only happened to see it by chance. But what he saw made him very interested, and he soon read the whole thing.

I WAS A WEAKLING, said the advertisement. **PEOPLE USED TO KICK SAND IN MY FACE. THEN I SENT OFF FOR MR WORLD'S MUSCLE MACHINE (PATENT PENDING) AND ALL THAT CHANGED. NOW NOBODY WOULD DARE KICK SAND IN MY FACE!**

Gordon was fascinated. What was a muscle machine, and how did it work? Was there a machine that could really

4

make you stronger? Surely not! And
yet there was only one way to find out,
and that was to try it.

At the bottom of the advertisement
was a form. If you filled in the form
and sent it off with the right amount of
money to Mr World, he would send
you the machine within three days.
What was more, if the machine did not

make a difference within two weeks, then you could send it back and your money would be refunded. Mr World guaranteed that.

Then there were several photographs of Mr World. In one, he wore nothing but a pair of swimming trunks and you could see all his muscles, bulging and rippling like a range of hills. In another, Mr World was shown pulling a railway carriage along a railway track, surrounded by applauding onlookers. Gordon could hardly believe it, but there it was in black and white.

Gordon rushed upstairs and counted out all the money in his money box. It was just a little short of what the muscle machine cost. He sat on his bed and stared at his feet, bitterly disappointed. He really wanted a

The incredible Mr World!

muscle machine and now he would never get one. It's not that he wanted to pull trains, or even to look like Mr World. All he wanted was to be fairly strong, or at least strong enough to stop a bully.

That night, as he lay in bed, Gordon looked at the advertisement again. He laid it down, turned off his light, and was just about to drift off to sleep when the idea came to him. Yes! Why not? Mr World looked like a friendly sort of person (in spite of all those muscles). He would send him what money he had, along with a letter promising to pay him the rest later on, when he had had time to save.

The following day Gordon did just that, and for the next three days he eagerly awaited the arrival of the postman each morning. There was nothing the first day, nor the second, but on the third, just as Mr World had promised, there was a large box, all stamped and tied up with string, and addressed to Gordon.

With eager hands Gordon opened

the parcel. Just inside the wrapping there was a letter, and Gordon read this before he went any further.

"Dear Gordon," the letter said, "Here is your muscle machine, which comes to you with the **strongest** best wishes of Mr World. Don't worry about the rest of the money. You can have this machine at a cut price, and I hope that it makes a real difference to your life. I'm quite sure it will! Remember one thing, though. Really strong people don't boast about their strength. That's important. Yours muscularly, Walter World."

Gordon was delighted. How kind of Mr World to give him the machine cheaply! But now there was no time to waste, and he set to unwrapping the machine so he could begin to use it.

The muscle machine was very intriguing. It was a long silver bar,

with springs and straps attached. You wound the straps around your arms, linked the springs to the end of the straps, and then you pushed and pulled as hard as you could.

It was hard work, and Gordon felt exhausted after only five minutes. He rested for half an hour – just as the instruction booklet said he should – and then he began again. After two sessions he stopped, and put the muscle machine away in his cupboard.

"Don't be impatient," said the instruction booklet. "Muscles don't grow in one day. Take it bit by bit, and you'll be surprised at what happens!"

Chapter 2

FOR THE NEXT five days, Gordon
practised regularly with the muscle
machine. The springs made a strange
noise while the machine was being
used, but by closing his door, Gordon
was able to do the exercises without
anybody knowing it. He was
particularly keen that his older
brother, Bill, should not get to hear
about what he was doing, as Bill often
laughed at him. He knew that Bill
would find the muscle machine a joke,
and pour scorn on him for using it.

On the fifth day, Gordon decided to

see if the machine was making any difference. His father was building a rockery in the garden, and Gordon had noticed that a large pile of rocks had been delivered for this. In fact, his father had complained that the rocks had been put in the wrong part of the garden and that he would have to spend a whole weekend carting them to the right place in his wheelbarrow.

"I don't know if my back's up to the strain," his father said. "They're terribly, terribly heavy."

Now Gordon stood before the pile of rocks and looked for the biggest one. One of them stood out from the rest. It was about the size of five footballs, and looked very heavy indeed.

"Right," said Gordon, gritting his teeth. "Let's see what I can do."

He had no confidence in being able to lift the stone, but he thought he would try anyway. After all, he had been using the muscle machine correctly, and Mr World had promised him that it would make a difference.

Gordon put his arms around the great rock. It was bigger than he had expected, and his arms just reached all the way round. Then he steadied himself, closed his eyes, and lifted.

Nothing happened. The rock sat exactly where it was, as if glued to the ground.

"I knew it wouldn't work," Gordon muttered to himself. "There's no such thing as a machine to make muscles. You're either strong or you aren't!"

But something inside him told him to try once more, so he crouched down again and encircled the rock with his

arms. This time he lifted it the right way, using his knees and not his back to take the strain.

"He . . . eeeave!" he said through gritted teeth. "Uuu . . . up!"

And with a sudden bump the rock came up, as if the glue holding it to the ground had melted. Gordon now stood quite straight, with the giant rock in his arms, and, what was more, it felt almost weightless!

With hardly any effort at all, Gordon walked with the rock over to the place where his father was building the rockery. He let it go there, and it fell with a resounding thud. Then he went back to the pile of rocks and picked up the next biggest one. That was even easier, and within a few minutes the entire pile of rocks had been carried from one place to another.

Gordon stood and looked at what he had done. He was quite astonished with himself, and he wondered if he had been imagining things. But no, it had really happened – he had moved a large pile of rocks with his bare hands. There was only one conclusion to be reached. He was now immensely strong. The muscle machine had worked.

Gordon's father was astonished when he saw what had happened to the pile of rocks.

"I can't believe it," he said to the family. "I've just been out in the garden and noticed that all those rocks have been moved across to the right place."

"Perhaps the people who delivered them did it," suggested Gordon's mother.

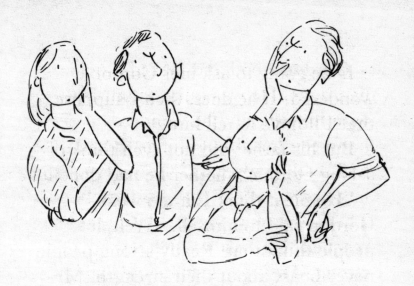

His father shook his head. "Impossible," he said. "I hadn't even told them that they were in the wrong place."

There was silence. His father looked at Gordon's older brother.

"Bill?" he asked. "You didn't move all those rocks, did you? It was very good of you if you did."

Bill smiled. "They looked far too heavy for me," he said. "No, I didn't do it."

Is he going to ask me? Gordon
wondered. If he does, then I suppose
that I'll have to tell him.

But his father did not even think of
asking Gordon whether he had done it.

"He must think I'm too weak,"
Gordon said to himself. "Well, let
people think that! Really strong people
never boast about their strength, Mr
World said. And now, I suppose, I'm
really strong!"

Chapter 3

GORDON CONTINUED TO use the muscle
machine, and now he really began to
feel the difference. When he put on a
shirt and clenched his fists, the shirt
would seem far too tight.

"It's all those muscles," he decided.
"It's exactly what the instruction
booklet said would happen."

He did not test his strength again for
a little while, but a few days after he
had moved all the rocks his chance
came.

It happened at school. Gordon had
not seen Ted for some time, but that

day as he was walking about in the schoolyard with his friend Michael, Ted came running up.

"Hey you!" he said to Michael. "I don't like the way you're looking at me."

"But I wasn't looking at you," protested Michael.

"Are you calling me a liar?" said Ted roughly, grabbing hold of Michael's shirt.

Gordon took a deep breath. The time had come to test the muscle machine again. As he breathed in, he felt his shirt getting tighter. In fact, one of the buttons popped off with the strain. Well, that was a good sign!

"He's not calling you a liar," Gordon chipped in. "But I am!"

Ted let go of Michael and turned angrily to face Gordon.

"Just you say that again," he hissed.

"Certainly," said Gordon calmly. "Not only are you a liar, you're a bully. And nobody likes bullies like you."

Ted went red in the face. Then, his eyes narrowed, he lunged forward and thumped Gordon in the chest with his two fists.

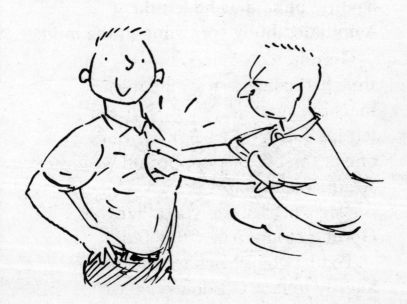

Gordon hardly felt a thing. As Ted hit him, he reached forward, took hold of Ted's two flailing fists, and lifted him up in the air. Then, as the astonished bully kicked and struggled helplessly, Gordon walked calmly over to the edge of the schoolyard and dropped Ted into a patch of mud.

"And don't try to bully anybody again," he said as he left the humiliated bully sprawling in the mud.

"If you do, you'll have me to reckon with."

Word of what had happened soon spread throughout the school. By that afternoon, Gordon had become a hero. Everybody was delighted, of course, as they were fed up with Ted's bullying ways and they had been longing for somebody to deal with him, but nobody had expected it to be Gordon.

Gordon was quite modest about it all. He said nothing about the muscle machine, even to Michael, and when asked about Ted he merely said, "It was nothing much really. Anybody could do it."

But everybody knew that this was not true and that Gordon must have grown immensely strong – somehow or other.

At home, nobody heard of what had

occurred at school, and the mystery of the rocks remained unsolved. Gordon's mother was a little bit suspicious that something odd was happening, but she couldn't work out exactly what it was.

"Your shirts seem to be losing their buttons," she said to him one day. "Is somebody pulling them off?"

"No," said Gordon, quite truthfully. "Nobody's pulling them off."

"Well, I shall have to sew them on more securely," his mother said. "Better still, I should teach you how to do it."

Gordon looked thoughtful. He was happy to learn how to sew on his own buttons, but he was worried about the needle. Now that he had become so strong, would he bend it as soon as he picked it up? He was not at all sure.

Although his mother had not

guessed, soon something was to happen which was to make Bill realise just how strong his brother had become.

Bill, who was old enough to drive, had an ancient red car, of which he was very proud. It often went wrong, though, and he seemed to spend a lot of his time fixing it, or being towed to garages. Yet in spite of this, he was very pleased with his car and loved to take his friends for rides in it.

One evening Bill came into the house, his face long with misery.

"I hit a lamp post," he said sadly. "I'm sure that it wasn't there when I first turned the corner."

"Is your car damaged?" asked Gordon.

Bill sighed. "My poor car . . . it'll never be the same again."

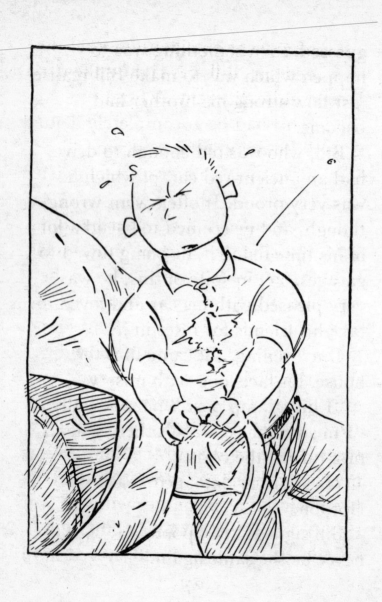

Gordon went outside to inspect the damaged car. Bill was right – the car looked quite different. A front mudguard had been completely dented in, and the bumper on that side seemed no more than a piece of twisted metal.

Gordon wondered whether he could help. Holding the bumper and bracing himself against the side of the car, he gave the strongest tug he could manage. There was a squeaking sound, followed by a crunching noise, and then, slowly at first but then more quickly, the bumper began to straighten out. Gordon tugged and twisted the metal until the bumper was in exactly the shape in which it had been before the encounter with the lamp post. Then, turning to the mudguard, he pushed and shoved until that was restored to its proper shape as well.

Standing back, Gordon dusted his hands and studied the car. You really couldn't tell now that it had had an accident at all.

Just as he was admiring his handiwork, Gordon became aware of somebody standing behind him. It was Bill, and his face was a picture of astonishment.

"Gordon . . ." he began. "Did you really do that?"

Gordon had to admit that he had fixed the car, and was straight away asked by his astounded brother how he had done it.

"Oh, I just pushed and pulled a bit," he said casually. "It wasn't difficult."

Bill looked sideways at his brother,

his gaze moving to the muscles in
Gordon's arms.

"You must have become very strong
all of a sudden," he said suspiciously.
"What have you been up to?"

Gordon did not answer the question.
He still did not want anybody to know
about the muscle machine.

"I'm glad that you're pleased with the repair," he said. "I'm happy to help any time you need me."

And with that, Gordon left Bill standing looking at his car, wondering exactly what his younger brother's secret was.

Chapter 4

GORDON WAS NOW halfway through
the programme of exercises set out in
the instruction booklet. He used the
muscle machine every day, but not for
more than fifteen minutes at a time.
His shirts were now far too tight for
him, but he had solved that problem
by cutting slits down the sides of the
arms. In that way, his muscles could
flex without bursting any buttons.

His mother, though, became even
more puzzled.

"First all those buttons go," she
said. "Then all your sleeves seem to

have split. Gordon, are you bursting out of your clothes?"

"Yes," said Gordon. "I think I am."

"Well, you shall have to eat a little less," said his mother. "Fewer ice creams and things like that!"

This disappointed Gordon, but he was still quite happy being strong. It's not that he had to use his great strength very often – certainly nobody had any further trouble from Ted since Gordon had dumped him in the mud. But it was good to know that the strength was there if needed.

Then something happened which was to test even Gordon's amazing new muscles. It happened, as these things often do, in an unexpected place and at a quite unexpected time.

Gordon's mother had asked him to go to the supermarket to buy a few groceries for her. She had given Gordon her list and some money. He always enjoyed walking round the supermarket, looking at all the tempting things stacked on the shelves.

He was standing looking at some boxes of porridge, noticing the picture on the boxes of a very strong Scotsman hurling a large hammer into the air – just like me, he thought – when he spotted that an old lady was standing on the tips of her toes, trying to reach a tin on a high shelf. Gordon was wondering whether he should help her when he saw her step up on to the first shelf to be able to reach a bit higher.

It was a bad mistake. As she put her weight on the shelf, the whole stack of shelves started to topple over towards her. The shelves were very high, and very long, and piled to the very top

with heavy things. If they fell, anybody under them was bound to be crushed.

Gordon gasped as he saw what was happening. The old lady had now fallen over, and was directly below the tottering shelves. If nobody did anything, then she would stand no chance.

For a moment or two he did not know what to do. Should he snatch the old lady from out of the path of the toppling shelves? Or should he try to stop the shelves from crushing her?

There was no time to move the old lady, as the shelves had now started to fall. So, wasting no more time, Gordon reached up and took the whole weight of the shelves on himself. There he was, standing like a statue, holding up the shelves while the old lady crawled away from the danger.

There were screams and shouts from the other shoppers. Somebody else seized the old lady and dragged her to safety. The manager of the supermarket had arrived now and he and his assistants looked on in astonishment as Gordon very gently and very slowly lowered the shelves to the ground. Of course all sorts of things had toppled out of them, and tins and jars lay scattered all about. But at least nobody was hurt, and that was the important thing.

As Gordon stood there, he was immediately surrounded by people slapping him on the back and trying to shake his hand.

"You're a hero!" they said. "That was amazing!"

"Stand back! Stand back!" called the manager as he marched up to

Gordon's side.

"Young man," he said, "that was
the most remarkable act of bravery I
have witnessed in all my twenty five
years as a supermarket manager. Well
done!"

Embarrassed by all the fuss, Gordon
was led off by the manager and taken
to the manager's office. There he was

sat in a chair and given a large glass of orange juice.

"I shall telephone the newspapers immediately," said the manager. "They will send their photographers to take a photograph of the old lady, and the shelves, and yourself. You'll be famous."

Gordon tried to protest.

"But I don't want to be famous," he said. "I was only trying to help. Anybody would have done the same."

"Nonsense," said the manager. "What you did was quite remarkable. No ordinary person could have done it."

Gordon realised that it was pointless to argue. The manager had made up his mind. So he stood up and started to leave the office.

"Where are you going?" asked the manager anxiously.

"I'm going to leave," said Gordon. "I don't *want* to be in the newspapers. I don't *want* to be famous."

"How ridiculous," said the manager. "You can't possibly leave before the newspapers have arrived."

Gordon tried to protest further, but he was too late. As he spoke, the

manager slipped out of his door and
slammed it behind him. Gordon tried
the handle, but it would not open. In
his excitement, the manager had
jammed the door!

Chapter 5

GORDON SAT GLUMLY in the manager's chair, waiting for the newspapers to arrive. He was not looking forward to all the fuss. And he was sure that people would ask him how he had become so strong, and if they heard all about the muscle machine then that would be in every newspaper. He remembered Mr World's advice not to boast: he did not want to let him down, particularly since he had so kindly sent him the machine for less than its real price.

He looked about the room, now his

prison. There were pictures of tinned food and vegetables on the wall. There were photographs of the manager opening a large can of beans. Then he noticed the window, high up on the wall, but not so high that it could not be reached by standing on the desk.

There was one problem, though. There were bars on the window, designed to stop people breaking in. But could they keep somebody from breaking out – especially if that somebody was strong enough to twist the bars?

Gordon climbed up on the manager's desk and took hold of the bars. It was not easy, as they were made of the strongest steel, but after a bit of panting and pushing, they bent. And there in the middle was a gap which was perfectly big enough for a

45

boy to squeeze through, even a boy
with big muscles.

Once outside, Gordon found himself
looking down at the supermarket
car park. He had to jump from the

window, and, as he rose to his feet afterwards, he saw a man and a woman staring at him from their car.

Suddenly the man wound down the window and shouted out at the top of his voice, "Stop thief!"

Gordon looked about him, puzzled. Was there a thief about, and, if so, where was he? Then he saw the man leap out of his car and come running towards him. He realised then what had happened. The man had seen him climbing out of the window and had decided, quite understandably, that he was a thief.

Gordon did not know what to do. If he explained to the man what had happened, the manager would be summoned and he would tell him that Gordon was no thief. But if he did that, then the newspaper people would

find him after all, and he did not want
that.

There was only one thing to do.
Gordon turned on his heels and began
to run out of the car park and into the
narrow delivery lane that ran along the
back of the supermarket.

It was a mistake. As Gordon ran
along the lane, with the man chasing
him, still shouting, he saw that the end
was blocked off by a high wooden
fence. He had run into a dead-end, and
his pursuer was closing on him
quickly. There was no escape.

Or was there? As he stood before the
fence, which was far too high to climb,
Gordon realised that there was a door
in it. It looked very firmly shut, but
this was no problem for somebody as
strong as Gordon. He took a deep
breath, feeling the muscles swell

beneath his shirt. Even with the slit arms, a button popped somewhere. Then, clenching his teeth, he put all his weight against the door and gave it a hefty shove. That should do the trick, he thought.

It did – but not in the way which Gordon had imagined. Instead of just opening the door. Gordon's great strength made the whole fence teeter for a moment and then come down with a crashing thud.

There was the sound of splintering wood. There was the sound of falling posts. Then, as an astonished gasp came from somewhere behind Gordon, the fence collapsed entirely, to lie about Gordon's feet like a pile of matchwood.

Gordon looked behind him. The man who was following him had

turned on his heels and was running as
fast as he could in the opposite
direction. He was no longer shouting,
"Stop thief!": now he was shouting,
"Help! Help!"

Gordon decided that it was time to go. Cautiously he peered around before he walked off, as if nothing had happened. Fortunately there were no newspaper men to record the great feat of strength he had just performed. And as for the man who followed him, would anybody believe him if he said that a high, stout wooden fence had been broken into a thousand pieces with one push from a mere boy? He thought not.

Gordon was wrong. The next day the newspapers had the whole story, printed boldly across the front pages.

"Who is the mystery strong boy?" they wrote. "Can anybody identify the shy hero who yesterday saved an old lady from certain death and then ran away before he could be properly thanked? The supermarket will pay a

LARGE REWARD for information
leading to the discovery of this
extraordinary young man who can
twist iron bars and destroy *brick walls*
with one blow!"

Brick walls? exclaimed Gordon.
That was typical of the newspapers.
They loved to exaggerate. But he was
worried by the story, and he feared
that sooner or later people would begin
to suspect that the person who picked
up Ted and dumped him in the mud,
who fixed dented cars with his bare
hands, and who saved old ladies from
falling shelves was one and the same
boy.

Chapter 6

MEANWHILE, AT SCHOOL, Gordon had
been careful not to do anything which
would draw attention to his strength.
People had stopped talking about the
fixing of Ted, and Gordon hoped that
sooner or later they would forget about
it altogether. Then came the human
pyramid, and Gordon found once
again that he was the centre of
attention.

It all began in a gym lesson. Mr
Ramble, the gym teacher, was
preparing a team for a gymnastics
competition and had decided that one

of the entries would be a human pyramid.

"It's quite simple," he explained to the class. "We get five people to stand on the ground. Then four people stand on their shoulders. Then three stand on the shoulders of the four, and two on the shoulders of the three. You end up with one person at the top. Do you understand?"

Everybody nodded.

"But what about those on the bottom?" somebody asked. "Won't it be a bit hard for them?"

Mr Ramble smiled. "Yes," he said. "It's particularly important that we have a strong person in the middle of the bottom layer. Any volunteers?"

Everybody shuffled their feet and looked elsewhere. Then somebody spoke.

"Gordon's the one," she said. "He's the strongest person in the school."

"Well?" he said. "How about it, Gordon?"

Gordon did not know what to do. He could refuse, of course, but that would be a bit unfair on everybody else. So, reluctantly, he agreed, and took his place in the middle of the bottom row.

Of course it was easy for Gordon. He didn't mind bearing the weight of everybody else, and the others in the bottom row found that they could transfer all the weight off their shoulders on to his. Mr Ramble was delighted. He could see that Gordon was holding the whole pyramid up, and he was most impressed.

Then Gordon did an extraordinary thing: he moved. Normally, if

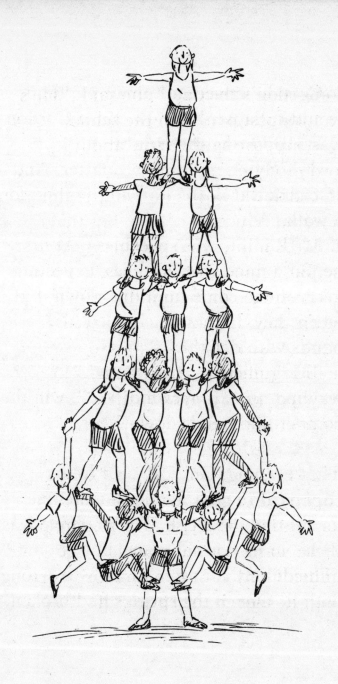

somebody moved, a human pyramid would collapse, but now, since Gordon was supporting the weight of everybody else, it did not matter. And so Gordon took the human pyramid for a walk.

Mr Ramble was speechless. At first he put a hand over his eyes, expecting everyone to come tumbling down, but when they did not he clapped his hands with delight.

"Magnificent!" he shouted. "A walking human pyramid! We'll win the competition hands down!"

That evening, Gordon went to his cupboard to get the muscle machine for his daily exercise. The machine was there, in its normal place, but he saw immediately that something was wrong with it. One of the springs had broken,

58

and another was twisted, and when
you began to use the machine it
croaked and groaned and refused to do
what it normally did.

Gordon wondered what on earth
could have happened. He had put the
machine away the previous evening in
perfect working order. Nobody ever
opened his cupboard – his mother
refused to do so (because of the mess)
and his father hardly ever came into
his room. So who else could it have
been?

Bill! Gordon felt a surge of anger
come over him. It must have been his
brother. He could never resist the
temptation to fiddle with machinery,
and he had obviously tried to work out
what the machine did just by using it.

Gordon stalked through to Bill's
room. His brother was sitting in his

chair and Gordon knew at once from the look on his face that he had been right to suspect him.

"My machine . . ." Gordon began.

Bill raised his hands in the air.

"I'm sorry," he said. "I'm really sorry. I just thought that I'd give it a little try."

"Well, you've broken it," said Gordon, still feeling furious.

"I know," confessed Bill, looking miserable. "I'm very, very sorry."

Gordon began to calm down. His brother clearly regretted what he had done, and he supposed that he could not help himself from being so inquisitive.

"What is it anyway?" asked Bill. "Is it a pogo stick?"

"No," said Gordon. "It's a muscle machine."

Bill was silent for a moment, and then he smiled.

"So it's you," he said. "I thought it might be."

"What do you mean?" asked Gordon.

"You're the mystery strongman," crowed Bill. "I suspected it might be you, and now I know."

Gordon looked at his brother for a while. Then he spoke.

"Did I fix your car?" he asked.

"Yes," said Bill. "You did."

"Then you owe me a favour," Gordon said quickly.

Bill looked warily at his brother.

"What do you want?" he said.

"I want you to keep quiet about the muscle machine," said Gordon. "And I don't want you to tell anybody that I saved the old lady in the supermarket."

Bill looked disappointed.

"I suppose so," he said reluctantly. "If that's what you really want."

That night, Gordon and Bill tried to fix the muscle machine. Bill fetched his tool kit from his car and extracted all sorts of screwdrivers and spanners. Together they took the muscle machine to bits, oiled it, and tried to straighten out things which looked as if

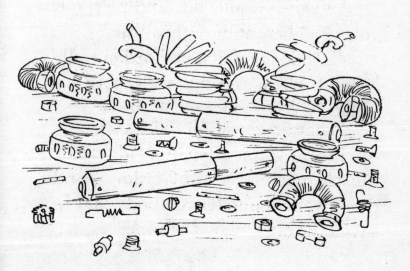

they needed straightening out. Then they reassembled it and Gordon tried to see if it would work. Unfortunately, it was now even worse. Nothing moved; it had jammed solid, and, what was more, Gordon noticed that there were some parts left over.

"No wonder it won't work," he complained. "Look at these."

They tried taking it to pieces again and putting it together, but once again there were various bits and pieces left over – different ones this time.

"It's no good," said Gordon sadly. "It's broken, and that's all there is to that."

Chapter 7

THE NEXT DAY Gordon wrote a letter.

"Dear Mr World," he wrote. "You may remember that a little while ago you sent me a muscle machine. I'm happy to say that it worked well, and I am now remarkably strong. I have also been most careful to follow your advice and not to boast about my strength. Unfortunately, my brother Bill, who has always fiddled with things, interfered with the machine and broke it. He says that he will buy me a new one next month, when he gets the money. So will you please reserve one

in my name and I shall send the
money as soon as Bill gives it to me."

Bill posted the letter for Gordon the
next day, and Gordon anxiously
waited for a reply. At last it came – in
the shape of another beautifully-typed
letter from Walter World himself.

"Dear Gordon," wrote Mr World.
"I was very pleased to hear that the
muscle machine achieved such good
results. I was also delighted to hear
that you have been modest about your
strength. That's exactly how it should
be! Strong people (really strong ones)
never have to throw their weight
about. But just let somebody kick sand
in their face, then that's another
matter!

"Now, I was sorry to hear that your
brother broke the muscle machine.
Sadly, I cannot reserve another one for

you for the simple reason that *you got the very last one I ever made*. Yes, if you had written one day later, it would have gone. You were just in time.

"You see, I'm quite old now – the photographs in the advertisement were taken long ago – and I decided to retire. It's hard work being a strongman, and, to be honest, I've had enough. I've built enough muscles. I've pulled enough trains. Now it's time to sit in trains and let somebody else pull me. So I've closed my business down.

"Now that you no longer have a muscle machine, may I offer you some advice? Without regular use of the machine, you will become weaker. I'm sorry, but that's the truth. All I can suggest is that you eat a great deal of spinach. Spinach makes you strong –

everybody knows that. It's full of iron,
I believe.

"So if you want to keep at least some
of your strength, then spinach it must
be. And, oh yes, I almost forgot
porridge. Look at the Scots. Look how
strong they are, always tossing cabers
around and throwing hammers. They

don't have muscle machines, and so it must be something to do with the porridge they eat every day.

"Good luck, Gordon! Yours sturdily, Walter World."

Gordon read the letter through with a sinking heart. So that was the end of the muscle machine and, unless he was careful, that was the end of his strength. He would be sorry to say goodbye to his new muscles. He would have to sew his shirts up again and keep out of Ted's way. And then there was his part in the human pyramid . . .

The human pyramid! If he lost his strength, then the human pyramid would come tumbling down about his ears. It would be so embarrassing, not to say painful. And poor Mr Ramble – he was pinning so much hope on winning the gymnastic competition. It would be a bitter disappointment for him.

Gordon looked at the letter again. Mr World did not say he would lose *all* his strength if he no longer used a muscle machine, and he did say that spinach and porridge might help. Well, if that were so, then that is exactly what he would eat. There would be porridge followed by spinach, followed by more porridge, and more spinach after that.

Gordon stopped. He knew that his mother would never buy him porridge and spinach all the time, and so he would have to try to get his own supplies. But how could he do that? He would never have enough money to buy large supplies of the two strength-giving foods, and there was none of either in the kitchen, as far as he knew.

Then Gordon had an idea. There was a way after all. Porridge and spinach came from the supermarket, did they not? And had the supermarket not offered a reward for information leading to the discovery of the secret hero who had saved the old lady?

"So!" exclaimed the supermarket manager. "There you are after all!"

Gordon looked bashfully at the beaming manager.

"I'm very sorry I ran away," he said. "And I'm very sorry about your fence."

The manager clapped his hands together.

"And I'm sorry too," he said. "I should never have bothered you like that. I only wanted to say thank you publicly. And as for the fence, we were going to knock it down soon anyway and build a better one."

"Well, you can say thank you publicly now if you want," said Gordon. "I don't mind if you call the newspapers."

The manager shook his head.

"No," he said firmly. "I've given the matter more thought, and I realise that a private thank-you would be much better. Now, what can we possibly do for you?"

72

Gordon plucked up all his courage for the answer.

"Could you give me enough porridge and spinach to last . . ." He paused. Dare he ask? "To last for a year?"

The manager's eyes opened wide in surprise.

"Porridge and spinach?" he exclaimed. "A year's supply? What a very peculiar request."

"But that's what I'd really like," said Gordon, adding politely, "If you don't mind."

"Of course I don't mind," said the manager. "If that old lady had been hurt, it would have been terrible. And I would have got into no end of trouble too. People don't like to be squashed while they're doing their shopping, you know."

The manager called in an assistant who arranged for regular deliveries of boxes of porridge and tins of spinach to be made to Gordon's house.

"And keep the supplies going for two years," instructed the manager. "No, better still. Make that three years!"

Gordon gulped. Three years of spinach and porridge. Would it be worth it?

That afternoon, Gordon told his parents all about what had happened. They were astonished to hear the story.

"So that's what happened to your shirts," Gordon's mother said. "That's one mystery solved."

"And that's how the rocks were moved," exclaimed his father. "Well! Well!"

Meanwhile, at school, the preparations for the gymnastic competition were going on. Gordon managed the human pyramid the first day – he was still very strong – but the second day it seemed a bit more difficult. He ate a great deal of spinach that night, and had two helpings of porridge the next morning, and that seemed to make a difference.

When the gymnastic competition at last came round, Gordon felt very anxious indeed. He felt his muscles, anxiously squeezing them through his shirt, and there was no doubt about it – they were smaller. Would the porridge and the spinach be enough? He doubted it.

There was a huge crowd watching the competition and Gordon was shaking with anxiety by the time that it came for the human pyramid to be erected.

"Now, please don't let me down,"

Mr Ramble whispered to Gordon.
"This is going to be the biggest
moment of my career."

Gordon winced. "I'll do my very
best," he said. "I promise you that.
But I must admit that I don't feel at
all strong today."

"You can do it," encouraged Mr
Ramble cheerfully, but Gordon could
see that the gym teacher was secretly
worried that the whole thing would be
a disaster.

There was silence in the stadium as Gordon and his team stood in the middle of the ring and prepared to create the pyramid.

"One!" shouted Mr Ramble. "One, two, three, four – Up! Up!"

The second row of people jumped up, and tottered precariously before settling down.

"Next!" called Mr Ramble, looking anxiously at Gordon. "One, two, three! Up! Up!"

Gordon felt his shoulders sagging. "I've got to do it," he said to himself. "I can't let everybody down."

Now it was time for the next row to get up and the crowd buzzed excitedly.

"One! Two! Up! Up!" shouted Mr Ramble.

Poor Gordon felt as if his arms would break.

"I can't drop them," he muttered through clenched teeth. "I just can't."

Now the final person was to get up.

"One!" Mr Ramble's voice was squeaky with excitement. "Up! Up!"

With the pyramid complete, there was a hush from the crowd. They had been told that the pyramid would do something dramatic, but had not been told what it would be.

Every fibre of Gordon's body seemed to be aching. Every muscle, every bone, every joint within him was protesting, urging him to let go and collapse. But no! He would not do that. The thought of all that porridge and spinach he had eaten came back to him in a vivid picture. There were pots and pots of porridge – whole cauldrons of it. There were fields and fields of spinach – whole valleys of it. Would all

that be for nothing? No! It would not!

Gordon gave a great heave and took a step. The human pyramid wobbled and shook, but stayed upright. He took another step, and one more after that. He was doing it. The human pyramid was on the move.

The crowd could not believe it. They clapped and clapped and continued clapping right until the pyramid reached the other side of the stadium and everybody jumped down. Gordon just stood still for a moment, regaining what was left of his strength. I did it! he said to himself. It doesn't matter if I

never perform another feat of strength,
I did that for Mr Ramble and my
friends!

At the end of the competition, when
the prizes had been awarded and
Gordon had carried off the supreme
trophy, an old man came up to him at
the entrance to the stadium.

"Excuse me," he said, taking off his hat. "Are you by any chance called Gordon?"

Gordon nodded. The old man's face seemed familiar, but he could not quite remember where he had seen him before.

"Then may I introduce myself?" said the old man politely. "My name is Walter World."

The old man reached forward to shake Gordon's hand. His handshake was a very firm one.

"I'm delighted to meet you," said Mr World. "And, what is more, I'm proud of you."

"I owe it all to you," said Gordon. "If it hadn't been for the muscle machine, then I could never have done it."

Mr World smiled. "Ah yes, the muscle machine," he said. "That reminds me. There's something I have to give to you."

He reached behind him and handed Gordon a parcel.

"No need to open it until you get home," he said. "I think that you can probably guess what it is."

"A muscle machine?" asked Gordon, hardly daring to believe his luck.

"Yes," replied Mr World. "After I wrote to you, I decided that I would give you my own one. It's the first one I ever made. I don't need to exercise any more at my time of life, not now that I've retired."

"Thank you," said Gordon. "Thank you very much, Mr World."

"That's perfectly all right," said Mr World. "I know you'll always put your strength to good use."

"I promise you that," said Gordon. Then a thought occurred to him.

"Does this mean that I won't have to eat so much spinach and porridge?" he asked.

"Yes," said Mr World. "I wouldn't give it up altogether, though. The occasional bit of porridge and spinach is very good for you, and tasty too."

Gordon accompanied Mr World out to his car. To his annoyance, the strongman found that a bus had been parked in such a way as to prevent him from driving off. The bus was empty, and the driver was nowhere to be seen.

"Give me a hand, will you?" Mr World said to Gordon.

"Of course," said Gordon. "Gladly."

And together he and Mr World lifted up the back of the bus and placed it in a better position. Then Mr World got into his car, waved cheerfully to Gordon, and drove away.

Also in Young Puffin

MR MAJEIKA
and the
MUSIC TEACHER

Humphrey Carpenter

**"Music teacher? What music teacher?
I don't know anything about any
music teacher."**

It's a new term at St Barty's and the
school is in uproar. Awful noises come
from Class Three, angry parents fill the
school and poor Mr Majeika is really
frightened. Why? A new music teacher
is coming who plans to start a school
orchestra, and as only Mr Majeika
knows, Wilhelmina Worlock is
a witch!